To Owen & Kei,
with all my love—Papa
—K. G.

To Sam and Anna Belle . . .
welcome to the neighborhood!
—H. C.

AUTHOR'S NOTE:

I remember all my fond memories of my Aunt Olga reading
Over in the Meadow by Olive A. Wadsworth to me. The poem was
the inspiration for *Who's Who?* I would also like to express my love
and thanks to our gestational surrogate, Teresa Johnston, her
husband, Adam, and their two terrific children, Lily and Ben.

A Feiwel and Friends Book
An Imprint of Macmillan

Text copyright © 2012 by Ken Geist.
Illustrations copyright © 2012 by Henry Cole.
All rights reserved.
Printed in China by South China Printing Co. Ltd., Dongguan City, Guangdong Province.

For information, address Feiwel and Friends, 175 Fifth Avenue, New York, N.Y. 10010.

Library of Congress Cataloging-in-Publication Data
Geist, Ken.
Who's who? / by Ken Geist ; illustrated by Henry Cole. — 1st ed.
p. cm.
Summary: Illustrations and simple rhyming text introduce six pairs of animal twins
who moo, hop, swing, swim, flap, and hoot their way through the day.
ISBN: 978-0-312-64437-6
[1. Stories in rhyme. 2. Animals—Fiction. 3. Brothers and sisters—Fiction. 4. Twins—Fiction.] I. Cole, Henry, ill. II. Title.
PZ8.3.G277Who 2012 [E]—dc23 2011015699

Book design by April Ward

The artwork was created with acrylic paints and colored pencils on hot-press watercolor paper.

Feiwel and Friends logo designed by Filomena Tuosto

First Edition: 2012

1 3 5 7 9 10 8 6 4 2

mackids.com

Who's
Who?

Story by
Ken Geist

Pictures by
Henry Cole

FEIWEL AND FRIENDS ○ NEW YORK

Over in the barnyard
where the cows moo and moo,
lives a noisy little calf
and her loud twin, Blue.

MOO MOO
MOO

Over in the garden
where the flowers grew and grew,
lives a jumpy bunny sister
and her twin brother, Lou.

"We hop," said the two.

So they hopped and they flopped
where the flowers grew and grew.

Over in the jungle
where the wild winds blew,
lives a long-tailed monkey
and her wild sister, Lulu.

So they swung and they clung
where the wild winds blew.

Over in the pond
where the water sparkles blue,
lives a colorful shiny fishy
and his rainbow sister, Sue.

"Swim!" said the brother.

"We swim," said the two.
So they swam and they splashed
where the water sparkled blue.

Over in the cave
where you only see a few,
lives an itty bitty bat
and his tiny twin, Stu.

Over in the night sky
where the owls who and who,
lives a silly little owlet
and his twin brother, Drew.